A BULLY BLUEPRINT

SOLUTIONS FOR KIDS

Strategies to help parents and educators eradicate bullying behavior

CHERRYE S. VASQUEZ, PH.D.

ISBN-13: 978-1546465799

ISBN-10: 1546465790

Bullying/Social Issues

ABOUT THE AUTHOR

Cherrye Vasquez is a retired public-school administrator and an adjunct professor who has earned a Doctor of Philosophy in Curriculum & Instruction; a Master of Education in Special Education; and a Bachelor of Arts degree in Speech Pathology/Audiology.

Cherrye's areas of specializations are in Multi-Cultural education, Early Childhood Handicapped, Mid-Management and Educational Diagnostician.

The central focus of Cherrye's books is...**DIVERSITY IS HEALTHY AND BULLYING IS NOT!** The essential psychology driving her writings is for children to realize that being different is healthy, important, beautiful and never to be feared. Indeed, each of us is designed to be different and therefore, unique! That children should learn about one another's similarities as well as their differences is a value that Cherrye drives home in all of her essays and books. Indeed, diversity is what makes this country great, our schools vibrant, and the future of our country strong.

As an educator, mother, and author, Cherrye believes that adults and educators must act as role models by developing and encouraging an atmosphere of respect for children to emulate and thrive in. To this end, her books depict meaningful and strong scenarios of how to reduce bullying by encouraging a healthy respect for diversity.

Website: https://www.cherryesbooksthatsow.com

Facebook Fan page: Books That Sow Strength, Character & Diversity

PREFACE

When our children are ill, it is customary to take them to the clinic to see their pediatrician or family physician/doctor. Most do this annually as a preventive measure, or if there is a sudden medical need. Whatever the reason, it is the pediatrician's and/or family doctor's goal to diagnose and further treat our child's illnesses.

In my opinion, bullying, much like a bad virus, requires strategies, interventions and reforms to combat its ill effects, much in the same way as a bug needs antibiotics for infirmities to heal and prevent them from invading the body. Healing a child's space, mind and heart is the primary goal.

I've written **A Bully Blueprint: Solutions for Kids** using health-giving titles to provide parents and educators with familiar health-centered, but relatable terminology in an attempt to assist with therapeutic ideas for dismantling undesirable, inappropriate bullying behaviors.

TABLE OF CONTENTS

WHAT IS BULLYING?

Definition & Types of Bullying Behaviors

BULLYING CAN BE DEFINED AS A SINGLE SIGNIFICANT ACT AND/OR PATTERN OF ACTS OF THE FOLLOWING:

Verbal

- name calling, teasing, insulting, or threatening.

Physical

- hitting, kicking, scratching, pushing, stealing, hiding/destroying someone else's property.

Social

refusing to talk to or play with someone or purposefully excluding someone.

Cyber

using electronic communication such as computer, cellular phone *(texting)* to write mean, intimidating, demeaning or threatening messages about someone, or electronically broadcasting hurtful photo of or alluding to someone.

Religious

- using religion as a weapon in order to gain power over other(s) while trying to recruit them to believe in their own religious traditions/ways. Such individuals may also quote the bitble, but most times do not follow but tease those who do not believe. On the other hand, religious bullying can also be defined as nonbelievers who bully those who they deem as religious fanatics, or Christians.

Note: When one or more students direct bullying at another student by exploiting imbalance of power, engaging in written or verbal expression, expression through electronic means, or conduct that is physically harming, damaging a student's property, and/or placing their victim in reasonable fear or harm, sufficiently severe, persistent, intimidating, abusive, and threatening, these behaviors are deemed significant.

No student has the right to infringe on the rights of another student at school, or through electronic means.

EXPLANATION OF BENEFITS

Parents need to understand

Parents: Know your rights...

Bullying is no joke, and it's no dress rehearsal. Bullying is real and children who choose to exhibit these behaviors are not backing down without intervention. What if your child asks, *"Who will help me deal with the daily struggles I'm having with the school bully?"* I'll answer your child's question for you – **YOU** will help your child. ***Yes, you will stop – look and listen***!

Because we realize bullying behaviors occur daily in our nation's schools, we must stop, look and listen to our children and deal with the pressures these annoying and often frightening behaviors pose on their lives.

Parents and school officials understand that we have a huge responsibility. We must do ALL that we can to help our children, but not just the child being bullied. We must also reach out to the child's bully. Yes, we must and we can.

LET ME ASK THESE QUESTIONS...

As a parent, are you aware of anti-bullying laws and policies in place at your child's school? If so, how are these policies being enforced? If not, have you voiced your concerns and/or asked to work closely with school officials in an effort to create anti-bullying procedures at your child's school? Do you know if school officials at your child's school are clear about what actually constitutes bullying behaviors? If not, what are you waiting for?

Do you know if school officials have written anti-bullying policies and a campus plan of action? Have they disseminated their plan to parents? Are your main stakeholders (students) feeling comfortable and safe in the school setting? I hope so, because it's also your duty as a parent to ensure these policies are not only in place, but acted upon consistently and proficiently each and every school day.

It is a common dilemma about what constitutes bullying behaviors versus normal play, or even friendly horsing around. Remember, bullying behaviors are intentional and are repeated acts over time. The child bully intends to pose harm, and he/she usually does not plan on stopping. I know that you have these concerns too, so I'll share common signs of bullying you will need to observe.

SIGNS OF BEING BULLIED...

- Bullying younger siblings/cousins – taking his/her frustration out on others
- Sudden moodiness
- Emotional – crying/whining
- Poor eating habits or asking to eat as soon as he/she gets home – *bully takes lunch or lunch money and your child is hungry*
- Depression
- Torn clothes or mysterious bruises/scratches
- Isolating self from others – appearing lonely

- A change in grades – poor grades
- A sudden dislike for school
- Exhibiting unfounded anxiety
- Low self-esteem
- Complaint of illness – stomach aches, headaches
- Asking to stay home from school
- Signs of threats or suicide

If you have reason to believe your child is being bullied, *Stop, Look & Listen* – Take Action **NOW** – Do not delay!

Talk to your children. Ask about their school day. Ask if there is anything you should know. Whatever you are doing or are planning to do, STOP! Children must trust that you will drop whatever you are doing to see them through this crisis, need to know you are listening, that you hear their frustration(s) and understand the pain they're experiencing. It is helpful to repeat what you've heard them say to you, thereby acknowledging that you are really listening. Above all, let them know that you will be there for them 'at all costs'.

Documentation...

It is critical to document an event as soon as possible after its occurrence. In this manner, incidents are still fresh in your child's mind. Listen to your child's version of the bullying event(s) in specific detail and record it in writing and read it back to confirm the accuracy of it.

In following up, you must document *(date/time/names of those in attendance)* every conversation you have with school officials. Never wait to make these notes. Do it real time to ensure that all elements of such conversations are recorded accurately for future reference if needed.

YOU WILL WANT TO...

- maintain distinct records of each person's story, separated by tabs in a tablet or a notebook;
- keep your child's version separate from that of a school official to ensure that messages don't overlap, become confused or accidentally combined – it is your primary document;
- determine whether other students have been affected by the same bully or bullies who are attacking your child. If so, what are their names? Were there any witnesses to the incidents? Again, record their names;
- determine if your child remembers which class the other students are enrolled in;
- determine whether your child can identify the offender(s);
- encourage school officials to interview other children who may have been bullied;
- note dates, times and settings in all of your documentation;
- color-code verbal vs. behavioral actions to ensure that sharing information is more succinct and organized (Example: Yellow = verbal / Blue = behavioral).

Detailed documentation will greatly assist school officials in targeting bullying incidents and provide indicators on how best to resolve issues as they examine antecedents *(causes/variables that may have prompted the bully to react inappropriately)*, so that changes and individually tailored support plans can be implemented.

APPROACH SCHOOL STAFF IMMEDIATELY...

Bullying will not just stop on its own. Don't be afraid to approach school administrators without delay.

You might find some school officials and administrators to be territorial and assertive that they are the educational experts, and you are 'just a parent'. Fortunately, that is the exception and most officials are open appreciative of your role as parents. Since you are your child's greatest advocate, you will want to work collaboratively with school officials at the school in which your child is enrolled.

HERE ARE A FEW IDEAS ON HOW TO APPROACH THE ISSUES OF YOUR CHILD'S BULLYING EXPERIENCE...

Do your research. You can assist school leaders with ideas of how to bully shield and bully proof the school your child attends. Be sure you have valid information to offer.

Approach school leaders as if you are on their side. Do what you can to avoid creating an adversarial relationship between you and the people who have the power to help stop what is happening.

Let the school leaders know you are not only concerned about your child, but all children enrolled at the school. This will soften your approach thereby giving you greater lead-in for support and the next steps for your own child.

Begin speaking to the school counselor before working your way up the organizational chart – *Test the water, first.*

My own child was bullied at school when she was in the fourth grade. I spoke to the school principal directly. Due to budget cuts, this particular school had no assigned counselor. I approached the situation as a concern for the other child as well as my own child. I said, "Perhaps this young girl is having personal problems in her home-life that are making her feel angry." Other times I would say, "Sounds like this child wants to take charge and is a bit bossy. Perhaps she can be shown how to use her leadership skills in a more positive and productive manner." By using this approach with the school principal, I believe I softened the conversation, thereby gaining the principal's attention. It appeared the principal was more willing to hear me out.

But, there are times when the school will not help. Now What?

Before I address this problem, I want to urge parents to always gather as much information as possible about the school your child is enrolled in during the first week or two of the new school year. This is the time when the climate is still warm and friendly, and stress levels aren't heightened due to the pressures of trying to keep up with everyday school life. Know the district level office organizational chart and levels of administration assigned to your child's campus. Attempt to retrieve their contact information such as names, email addresses, voice mail, and telephone numbers, and perhaps location of their offices – this is last resort. Above all, never show up without an appointment.

When your child's school refuses to listen, take your complaint seriously or help you through a bullying crisis, and you know you have done your part by speaking first, to the classroom teacher, followed by the school counselor, assistant principal and principal if circumstances have taken you this far. If still unsuccessful, you should contact central office staff and speak to your child's school-assigned area superintendent. Bottom line – follow the organizational chart first. *Play fair!*

Share your concerns and let this individual know you have tried to work collaboratively with school officials at the campus level of your child's school. Trust me – Now that bullying has gained national attention, there is no doubt this person will be all ears.

At the time of this writing, there are approximately forty-eight (48) states that have laws mandating anti-bullying programs and services in schools, but some schools have been slow in implementing the programs.

Be sure you know the anti-bullying laws of your state ***(Bully Police, USA)*** has a state by state listing of anti-bullying legislation. Be ready and able to recite the Senate Bill and House Bill laws associated with the bully's offense, or take a copy of the law with you. For example, if you live in Texas and your child is experiencing sexual harassment issues at school, and no one will address the issue, share your knowledge of **Texas anti-bullying statutes Texas Education Code, Sections 25 and 37.** If you do this, everyone will know that you mean business!

When to call a lawyer...

If you have gone through all the recommended steps above, more than likely you will not have need to call a lawyer; however, there may be times when your story will land on 'deaf ears.' If no one will listen to you, or if everyone has listened to you and they have chosen not to intervene, there is no more time to waste. You will want to get legal advice immediately. Time is of the essence and the safety of your child is paramount!

Focus on your child...

Remember, there are effective steps you can take as your child's anti-bullying advocate. Consider the fact that bullying related bully-cides (*suicides stemming from bullying*) are real.

STOP whatever you're doing and act quickly on your child's behalf. Our children count on us to help them through times of crisis. Your child may have already tried to handle it alone and exhausted all strategies. This is not the time to put ANYTHING else before your child. Show your child that they can trust and count on you. You are the primary support person in their young lives.

PREVENTIVE MEDICINE

Begin with Legislators & School Board Members

We must begin at the top of the organizational chart as we depend on our legislators and then local school board members to regulate bully laws and anti-bullying policies in our school systems/districts.

Bullying is receiving world-wide attention especially where school districts are concerned. This pandemic is not only being handled by local campus school administrators/officials, but **school boards** are now adopting policies. That's right! We must know and understand the bully laws of the state in which we reside.

Beginning in the 2012-2013 school year, school boards were **mandated** to adopt policies and administrative procedures for their school districts.

TO PROHIBIT BULLYING, THESE POLICIES MUST...

- Prohibit retaliation against any person, witness, or another person who in good faith provides information regarding bullying;
- Establish a procedure for providing notice of an incident of bullying to a parent or guardian within a reasonable period;
- Establish the actions a student should take to obtain assistance and intervention in response to bullying;
- Set out available counseling options for a student who is a victim of, is a witness to, or engages in bullying;
- Establish reporting and investigative procedures;
- *Prohibit school officials from disciplining a student who is the victim of bullying, for the student's use of reasonable self-defense in response to bullying.

Due to **Zero Tolerance**, a Federal Gun-Free Schools Act of 1994, which derived from school districts being eligible to receive funds if they had a firearms policy, many school districts coined this term and used it within their discipline policy as a means to rid their schools of behavior problems. Any child with a discipline infraction regardless of the nature would have discipline consequences to bear.

EXAMPLE:

If a child being bullied *(hit, kicked)* on a daily basis attempted to defend him/herself by finally striking back, such child would be just as guilty of the behavioral infraction and could face discipline penalties just as severe as the perpetrator *(bully)*.

According to Wikipedia (2013) Zero tolerance is a policy of punishing any interpretation of rules, regardless of accidental mistakes, ignorance, or extenuating circumstances.

When I read these new school board policies I became relieved help is finally here for our children. Our children deserve going to school in peace.

School is a place to learn, not a place to be hit, kicked, slapped, or receive ill-treatment of any kind. *

Parents – Do you know if a bully policy has been established within your child's school district/school campus? If so, do you know if school officials revisit and tweak the policies on a regular basis? Do you know if the policy is being enforced? It's worth taking the time to investigate.

***Although I am pleased that new regulations are in place, I must admit to having had mixed feelings about a child being punished for defending him/herself against a bully as per zero tolerance, even though kindness is always the right objective.**

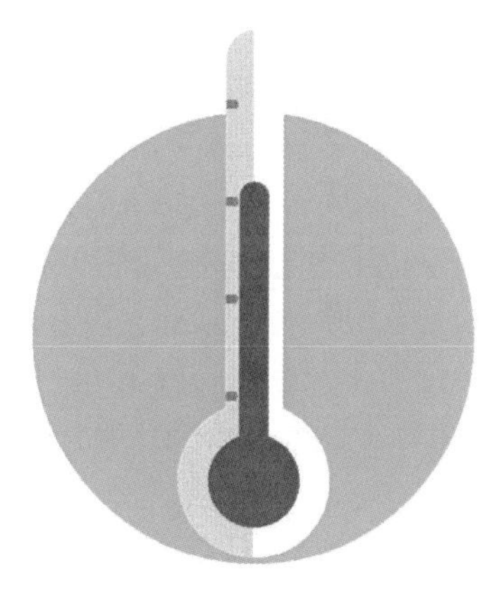

TAKE OUT THE THERMOMETER

WHAT'S REALLY GOING ON?

I am a firm believer that parents, educators and classroom teachers already know how to stop bullying behaviors. These important 'players' in the lives of children simply need to be reminded that they are the adults who are in the 'driver's seat' and can shape children's ideals and behaviors while they are still young, moldable and impressionable.

Yes, this is the time to gauge how a child interacts with others. *What is the reading on the thermometer? What is the child's temperature?* Don't be fooled. Learn the child's ways and actions when interacting with others.

We can deal with bullying behaviors when children are still young. We can teach children the 'golden rule' and we all know what that rule entails: *Treat others the way you'd want to be treated.* If this is true, who would bring harm to themselves?

It is within the duration of a child's primary years in life that we have control for shaping their minds and hearts. Throughout this very crucial time in a child's life we will want to instill deep-seated attitudes of care, appreciation and remorse for the feelings of others, especially their family members, siblings and playmates.

For the period of a child's formative years, parents can observe how their children interact with their dolls, pets, and friends on play dates and gain a sense of their temperament.

Parents, educators and classroom teachers will want to redirect inappropriate and unfavorable behaviors made by children and then talk with them about feelings and how their actions may impinge on their friends who could become upset by harmful words or inappropriate physical and perhaps harmful touch.

Adults should take the time to use such upsets as 'teachable moments.' Stop a child's inappropriate behaviors on contact and redirect the child at that exact instant. While it isn't necessary to place a child in uncomfortable embarrassing situations, adults should promptly remove the child and have a word with them in private. Do not delay!

HOW TO STOP BULLYING BEHAVIORS WHILE CHILDREN ARE STILL YOUNG...

- Use a calm voice to get the child's attention;
- Tell the child you'd like to have a word with him/her in private;
- Walk over to a quiet place with the child;
- Get down to the child's eye level and be sure to maintain eye contact between you and the child during communication;
- Tell the child what you observed;
- Pause a moment giving the child time to respond *(just in case you misinterpreted his/her intentions);*
- Ask the child how he/she might feel if their friend(s) reciprocated with the same actions/words toward them;

- Talk about feelings and caring for friends. You may want to use examples;
- Talk about maintaining friends and returning for future play dates;
- Make a mental note to yourself to model with the child at home/school, reiterating the importance of treating others the way he/she wants to be treated;

I believe strongly in the Proverb: *"Train-up a child in the way he should go, and when he is old, he will not depart from it."*

Feelings of remorse and care grow over time. If a child has never had feelings of regret, harvesting these feelings will be hard to produce as a child grows older into the age of accountability.

A COMPLETE PHYSICAL EXAMINATION

The Bully

Who knows really why a child bullies?

Is the child negatively acting out his/her pain?

Is the child not really in pain, but just being mean and enjoys seeing others hurt?

Is the child self-centered, or selfish?

Now you must investigate and find out - ***Why?***

There could be various reasons, and/or antecedents prompting, or causing these actions, and it's your job to explore determining the very root of the problem behavior(s). How did the behavior(s) originate? When did the behavior(s) originate?

We realize no child is perfect. Children get into things, have feelings, get angry, confused and endure mood swings just like each of us; however, the focus here is to determine what underlying factors may cause, or jumpstart ongoing, purposeful, inappropriate behaviors habitually targeted at others.

Now, let's assess inappropriate behaviors and get down to the core *(very root)* and main purpose of the problem behaviors you want to see diminished.

Ask yourself...

- What is the problem behavior? Have I pinpointed it?
- Where does the behavior occur?
    - home
    - hallway
    - lunchroom
    - classroom
    - between classes
    - playground
- When does the behavior occur?
    - Specify time of day *(8:15 a.m.) (3:21 p.m.)*
- Who are your team assistants?
    - Identify people who will know your plan of action
    - Identify team members who will consistently help carry out the plan at school (*nurse, teacher, counselor, etc.*) parents
- How will you gather pertinent data?
    - Chart

    - Graph
    - Journal
    - Notes (cell phone)
- How will you utilize the data once learned about the child?

Once the physical examination is completed, it's time to look further. Through a closer look *(observations)*, take note of behavioral patterns. *Analyze* what you've noted. Do you see a *pattern* of incidents during certain times of day, or places?

Note: If there are several behaviors you want to work on, always work on the most annoying one first. Take each behavior one step at a time.

Analyze, Observations and Patterns

Once team members have begun collecting important data, ensure they've developed a form to chart results.

For a shortened example, your form can look like the one below

Collecting Student Data

Student Name: ________________________

Focused Behavior: ______________________

Start Time: ________ End Time: ________

Scale: / = 0 + = 1

Days

Activity	Time	9/1	9/2			
	7:30-8:00					
	3:30-4:00					

Your collection of data may range over a few days *(determine how long is reasonably sufficient)*. You should begin to determine patterns regarding settings and times when behaviors mainly occur or do not occur. If you find patterns, pause to dissect determining variables that may have initiated, or influenced the problem behaviors. You can't move on to correct until you know exactly the cause – the root of the problem.

Be sure to pin-point decisive information determining the purpose of the unwanted behaviors you focused. Did you determine if the child was trying to...?

- Get attention?
- Escape from an issue?
- Tell you he was tired, or didn't get enough sleep the night before?
- Tell you he/she was hungry?
- Tell you he/she needed to talk to someone about an issue he/she was facing/experiencing?
- Tell you he/she needed a bathroom break?

Note: Your data collecting form should be designed and tailored for your needs. I would recommend 30 minute intervals from the time the child arrives at school until the end of the school day. If parents are using this form at home begin at the time the child wakes up until bedtime.

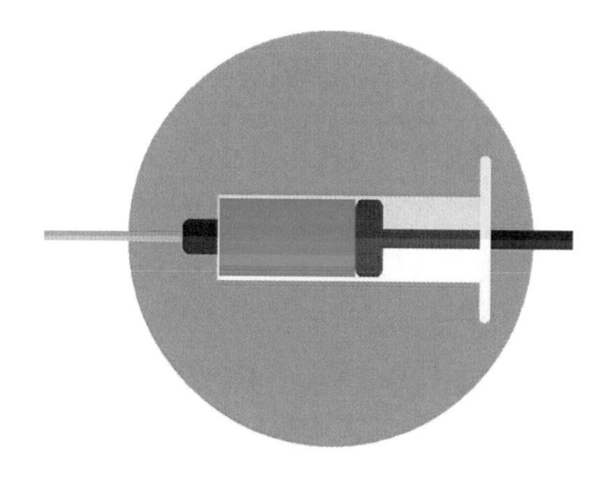

RECEIVING THE APPROPRIATE DOSAGE

IDENTIFYING CONCERNS

Now that you've targeted the *antecedents (variables that instigated the undesirable behaviors)*, what are you going to do with this information?

What have you discovered pertinent to eliminating or correcting the undesirable behaviors?

Remember, your goal is to help diminish these problem behaviors, and make the child-bully successful.

ASK YOURSELF THESE QUESTIONS:

- ▫ Did you find a time of day the negative behaviors presented themselves more than other times of the day?

- Does the child get frustrated in crowds (*lunch time, restroom, hallway, family gatherings and holidays)*?
- Does the child work better in smaller groups?
- Are there particular children this child works better with and perhaps has similar strengths that are positive?
- Does the child need a break between academics, jobs, activities?
- Does the child get excited when the adult gives positive rewards and/or attention during tasks?
- Does the child prefer to work on one activity over another? If so, how can the adult help the child transition from one task to another?
- Have all the child's personal needs been met *(hunger, restroom breaks, water)?*
- How is the climate of the room? Is there tension? Are there loud noises *(voice tone, loud air conditioner)?*
- How is the temperature in the room *(too cold, too hot*)?

If you've pin-pointed the variables causing the problem behaviors, how will you address these for the child's success? You must tie your data collection results to effective interventions that work. Now you must link your assessment results to the interventions you will put into practice.

What replacement behaviors will you offer the child?

EXAMPLES...

If from your data collection you observed the following:

1. The child gets irritable working for longer periods of the day,
    - You will want to work on a plan to give the child short breaks during the day or activity.
2. If the child has repeated outbursts...

- You will want to teach alternative ways to communicate in positive manners such as:
    - Getting the teacher's attention nonverbally by raising his/her hand *(the teacher immediately rewards the child):*
        - determine how rewards will look *(sticker, smile, verbal praise, drawing a picture, more play time)*
        - Holding up a picture *(break time, please)*
        - Determine if the rewards are age appropriate
        - Determine if the rewards excite the child to perform better

Before you can execute proper rewards, you must first get to know the focused child.

Ask yourself...

- Have you spent enough quality time with the child showing you genuinely care?
- Have you gotten to know the child?
- How is your rapport with the child?
- Does the child trust you?
- Do you know the child's interests, hobbies, talents? If not, you will not know which rewards best interest the child.

Be certain the replacement behaviors are in place and followed by all staff involved on the team working with the child.

Note: The above are just examples. You may find these do not address the needs in your data collection, so you must determine which replacement behaviors meet your desired outcome.

DISPENSING THE MEDICINE AT SCHOOL

School Officials

Instructional Leaders, Counselors, and Teachers must carry out the school-wide systematic behavioral plan set in place for school officials.

School-wide behavioral plans should be uniformly applied in the school setting. Children should have the same behavioral expectations throughout the entire campus. This includes the cafeteria and custodial employees who may have interaction with students, however minimal. These employees should have orientation and training on the school-wide behavioral plan.

Examples:

1. If the child is standing in the lunch line waiting to be served and is....
    a. Speaking loudly;
    b. Pushing/shoving peers;

c. Touching trays not his/her own or intending to use.

The cafeteria employee can be trained how to ask the child to use his/her inside voice, not to push/shove others, how to respectfully think of hygiene by not touching lunch trays others will eat from.

2. If the custodial staff is working and notices a child

   a. Running in hallway;

   b. Throwing litter on the playground or anywhere on school premises;

   c. Not returning lunch tray to proper location in cafeteria.

The custodial staff can be trained how to properly ask a child to refrain from running in the hallway, avoid throwing litter on playground, how to discard lunch tray properly *(compliance training).*

School officials can use staff development time to train staff *(trainer-of-trainer model or informally referred to as 'train the trainer' model).*

In addition, the bully-ee *(victim)* of the bully, can be trained and taught how to effectively tell the bully to stop.

EXAMPLE...

If a child-bully hits another child, tell the victim to walk a few steps away from the bully, and then tell the bully "stop." Immediately afterwards the victim should inform the teacher or adult in charge of monitoring the children.

Note: During staff development sessions, have meaningful discussions on how this looks for children.

KEEPING THE MEDICINE DOWN

Self-fulfilling prophecy & Self-esteem

'Practice makes perfect'...

Instilling deep-seated empowerment within is crucial today more than ever and can be an effective pivotal point for dismantling low self-esteem or low self-worth in our children.

How will you ensure a child's negative behavior won't return? So that a child does not relapse, it is imperative to instill a sense of purpose. It bears repeating that we can accomplish this simply by teaching children how to self-affirm while we shower them with positive, uplifting affirmations and self-fulfilling prophecy techniques, before you embark upon this journey.

AGAIN, ASK YOURSELF...

- Have you spent enough quality time with the child showing you genuinely care?
- Have you gotten to know the child?
- Do you know the child's interests, hobbies, talents? If not, you will not know which rewards best interest that child.

Each child has value and unique characteristics. They may need to have someone point these out to them, or assist with shaping and molding them, but the reality is it's there. It is our job to help them tap into it. Once you've assisted the child with highlighting his/her talents, each is on the right path toward building and reaching goals.

Most importantly, if we are effective in our mission, at risk children won't feel so isolated, contemplate suicide as an escape, and be less likely to become bullies or the targets of bullies.

As parents, we can work on these skills at home, and our teachers and administrators can *carry the torch* once our children are in their hands. Perhaps short social skills lessons will help.

What can you do to help with this undertaking? What ideas do you have? Remember, it takes the school and parents working together as a community.

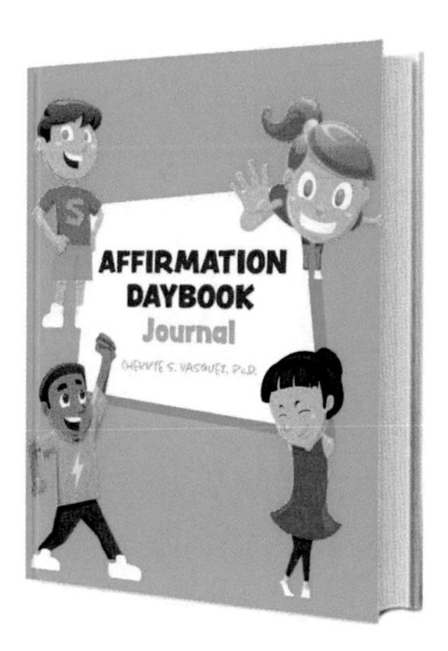

Resource: ***Affirmation Daybook Journal***

Link: https://www.amazon.com/dp/1469914573/ref=cm_sw_su_dp

I wrote this journal to help students build positive empowerment. Using this journal will help children build self-confidence and deep inner strength.

AN APPLE A DAY KEEPS THE DOCTOR AWAY

Effective Communication Skills

Teaching our children how to communicate effectively is one way to help solve and have peaceful connections with their peers. Effective communication helps soothe issues that may become explosive and/or annoying to the point of one child becoming agitated with another. Think of ways to help children conquer this goal.

As educators, adults, parents, and community leaders we must role model effective communication skills before children/students. We'd surely want our children to communicate effectively in classrooms and their communities.

How to teach effective communication...

Teach children,

- the importance of eye contact
- how to take turns listening to one another
- how to wait until it's their turn to talk
- how to let the speaker realize they are listening attentively
- how to ignore gossip
- how to make small talk engaging an introvert to talk with them
- how to get along with extroverts and those who monopolize the entire conversation
- how to negotiate ideas
- how to say "no" without being afraid
- how to use online communication devices appropriately without harming others instigating/promoting online bullying
- how to teach children how to agree to disagree
- how to listen to their peer's point-of-view even if it differs from their own
- how to incorporate daily journal writing

Teach children how to write reflection papers. This activity can be highly effective at soothing and calming them. Some children will readily write, while you may have to encourage others.

Allow the child to express his/her views. This will give children a sense of cause, and reflection. Tell the child that you value his/her opinions about current events, family traditions, even world views.

Tell the child you want to listen to his/her thoughts and opinions on various topics affecting them or others.

Tell children to respond using creative thoughts, artifacts, and aids of their choice.

Encourage children to make their responses as interesting and lively as they wish with the provision that their words must be respectful and not demeaning, harmful/hurtful to others.

Ensure children understand that communication may have many different, but interesting facets, that communication is a two-way transaction – listening and conveying.

Teach children the importance of listening attentively to others first, then share their thoughts on the matter at hand. Sharing and listening harvests respect.

Leaders must be able and prepared to role model appropriate ways of conversing. If we can do this as adults, our children will follow and take our example.

So long as students use friendly discourse as they dialogue one to another, and respect one another's sharing, the "sky is the limit."

One other point you will want to stress to students is this: You never have to subject yourselves to, or agree with another's thoughts and opinions, but it is always *kosher* to agree to disagree in friendly, kind and/or mature ways.

Teach children that whenever they communicate online, to practice 'netiquette' which means using polite words and good manners at all times. Netiquette is merely online etiquette. When we teach children how to converse online, exercising respect and consideration, they gain effective, non-harmful communication skills.

Rudeness, put downs and harsh words are not acceptable communication options. In fact, these are forms of bullying behaviors that should never be tolerated within an online community, network or discussion forums.

Teach students to reference another person's point-of-view/information in their world, and then do so. If such information does not fit their expectations and/or character, leave it alone. Perhaps one of their peers can/will benefit from such information.

Tell students that although they may think another's information is unworthy, it doesn't mean that others feel the same way.

Teach children they can learn from others and although it is okay to disagree with another's point-of-view, they should always try to understand what is being conveyed before "tuning them out." Give what their peers have to say a "fighting chance." Who knows, something enlightening might be expressed as a teachable moment, imparting knowledge and some helpful tips to consider.

Responding negatively using 'put downs' and other criticism is a 'no-no'. Effective communication is an art, and it takes maturity to understand that. Think about how great and respectful our classrooms would be if adults taught these skills to children.

Teach children how to use phrases as a segue for better understanding their peer's thoughts/points of view in kind, considerate, and socially appropriate ways.

Feel free to use cue cards for role modeling and student practice.

Teach students effective ways to probe their peers without bullying.

Probe further by stating/asking...

- "You said ..... Would you explain what you were referring to?" *(Be sure to use direct quotes. Never make false accusations, put words in someone's mouth, or summarize what you think they said in your own words)*
- Here is my take on your opinion...
- Once upon a time I...
- From my experience on the subject......
- I read an article once that suggested...
- Did you know that recent statistics reveal ...?
- Sounds interesting. Here's my stance on the topic...

- I don't exactly agree with your thought on this subject, but can we agree to disagree? Here's why...
- Have you ever thought about it this way?
- I've never thought of it that way
- Here's another way to think of it...
- I didn't want to interrupt you, but you said something that made me want to share this with you...

Finally, effective communication takes skill. If children are ever a part of group/forum discussions and their voices aren't being acknowledged, or if the group's moderator is insensitive, lacks the skills, professionalism and maturity needed to facilitate appropriately, tell children to kindly bow out and attach themselves to groups that are uplifting, empowering, and those making positive differences in the lives of others. There are any number of groups out there and the best among them value all input and ensure that *every voice* count. Remember, what children have to offer could make a positive difference in someone's life.

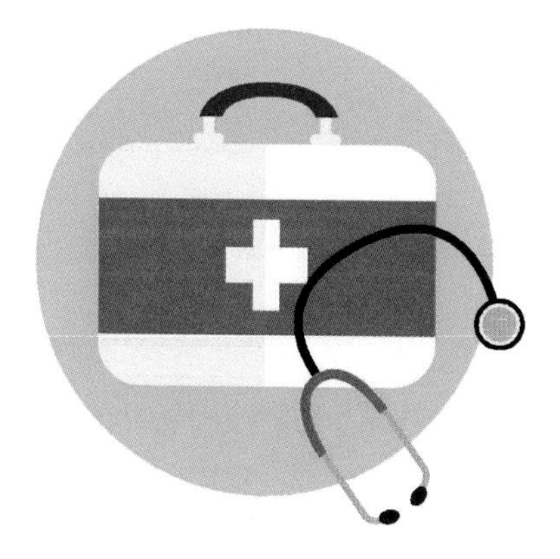

WHEN THE MEDICINE CABINET IS EMPTY

BUILDING LEADERSHIP SKILLS IN CHILDREN

Develop and maintain positive leadership skills-building in children. Yes, we can actually teach our children how to lead in positive, effective ways.

POSITIVE, EFFECTIVE LEADERSHIP WILL ACCOMPLISH TWO THINGS:

- Teach children how to interact positively with others; and
- Give children deep-seated empowerment allowing them to feel liberated.

Before continuing our work on reducing the incidence of bullying and suicide, it is of primary importance that our children feel good about themselves.

Steps to encourage a child's self-esteem...

- Teach children to believe in themselves and their accomplishments in life however big, or small;
- Instill a sense of positive self-identity. Children must love and own who they are;
- Tell children to repeat after you: 'I can do it!' or 'I did it!';
- Encourage children to never be afraid to attempt new ideas and tasks;
- Teach children that IT IS OKAY to question adults/teachers in courteous and positive ways. This builds self-confidence;
- Reassure children that IT IS PERFECTLY OKAY to make mistakes so long as they learn from them. Children must 'pick themselves up, dust themselves off, and start all over again' until they get it right;
- Teach children to 'keep going' and 'stick with' their goals. It's too easy to give up when things get tough, but there are brighter days ahead;
- Teach children that IT IS OKAY to say, 'NO' to a friend or acquaintance who pressures them to participate in unfriendly behaviors, or to say things they aren't comfortable with. Practice makes perfect and becomes easier over time.
- Thereafter, children must also learn how to positively and appropriately interact with family members, siblings, pets, etc.

What can parents/guardians do?

- During family gatherings, holiday gatherings, and play-dates, always monitor your child's behavior. Ensure that children are taught how to treat and care for others in a courteous and respectful manner;
- Teach your child how to take turns during game board playing, and sports activities;

- When you observe children behaving in unsociable and inappropriate ways, pause them for a moment and in a kind manner, attempt to redirect them to rethink how to treat others. Never embarrass them;
- It's okay to role-play positive behaviors with your child at home. The child will remember and will most likely emulate such positive behaviors outside the home;
- Carefully observe how children interact with pets and playing with dolls. Are they caring, loving, conscientious and capable of showing remorse? If not, this is a teachable opportunity.

Varying Personalities/Physical Traits...

Because children are born into diverse cultures, home environments, and of course, present different physical make-ups and traits, they are not the same. ALL children can learn effective leadership while accepting and admiring those who look and think differently than their personal norm, or of how they perceive their norm to be, or how they feel people ought to appear to them. Help children overcome 'status quo' ideologies.

We live in a society where privilege often obscures our judgment. Teaching children effective leadership communicates how to avoid showing partiality towards certain people and/or groups of people.

Definition of Diversity...

Diversity simply means an assortment or variety of something whether it is ethnicity, color, opinions, or more. Diversity encompasses much more than different foods, clothes and ways of life. Diversity may also mean different ways to enjoy recreation, family traditions, belief systems, religion, and languages.

So then, what should children look for?

- Belief systems

- Cultural traditions
- Various recreational differences
- Various Instruments/Sports
- Ideology/Opinions/Thought processes
- Languages
- Religion
- Schools/jobs
- Styles of homes/Where people choose to live
- Styles of clothing
- Choices of food types
- Communities
- Holiday traditions
- Celebratory traditions
- And more.

How can we teach children to appreciate and learn about other children?

Children can be...

- trained to initiate conversations with other children who do not share their same methods, approaches, lifestyles, traditions and practices;
- encouraged to include their peers in group activities *(clubs, school activities, parties);*
- encouraged to express themselves using personal journals and then share their cultural experiences with one another;
- encouraged to always show respect for their friend's difference(s);

- trained how to appropriately negotiate/compromise with friends and family members when in disagreement.

Being allowed to command a feeling of positive affirmation also enables children to possess 'feel good' personalities. Teaching self-affirmation and self-fulfilling prophecy skills and techniques are other ways to initiate the process of building the blocks of positive leadership. Children who feel empowered usually become the 'trailblazers' of tomorrow. It is our job to work with our children to teach how positive empowerment is expressed via actions, or words.

Where do we begin?

A child starts out learning how to develop socially appropriate and positive leadership skills from his parents or guardians. Thereafter, teachers can 'carry the torch' in the classroom setting to teach social skills lessons. Home/school relationships where parents and school officials work together are the ideal supportive partnership.

No-No (Stereotypes/Biases) ...

- Be careful not to project stereotypes. Adults must not harbor or express biased feelings or opinions lest they unwittingly convey such feelings to their children;
- Be careful about judging others. Teach children how to find positive attributes about others. What are 2-3 positive attributes you can find about someone?;
- Avoid racist and sexist and/or homophobic comments;
- Teach children the importance of respecting and treating others the way they'd want to be treated themselves;
- Teach children they do not have to believe in, or agree with the differing lifestyles, but they must not 'bully' their own ideas onto others;

- Let children know it is okay not to become followers *(peer pressure)*, but leaders instead;
- Parents may add 'diverse' artifacts to their homes for children to reflect upon and learn to appreciate ethnic diversity;
- Encourage children to read books with 'diverse' characters;
- Encourage children to read books about 'diverse' regions/countries, traditions, cultures and customs;
- Teach children that it is okay to break away from toxic groups without feeling guilty.

As parents/guardians/teachers/adult leaders, we can 'inspire' children to become positive leaders who appreciate diversity and differences, all in the spirit of guiding them toward developing positive, healthy relationships.

FOLLOWING THE DOCTOR'S ORDERS

Empowerment

'Empowerment' can be either negative or positive but for the purpose of this writing, we will focus on 'positive empowerment'.

Children must first love who THEY are. This means they must be able to self-identify in positive ways. Positive self-identity means knowing and loving who they are as individuals.

Defining Empowerment...

The process of becoming more confident, especially in controlling one's life and claiming one's own rights involves actions intended to grow a child's independence and self-sufficiency. An empowered child is able to self-rule with greater determination and represent self-interests in a responsible way without negative persuasion.

A critical element of empowering a child is to first get to know his/her likes, dislikes, personal interests in subjects and activities such as hobbies, sports and the arts. Being able to communicate on familiar ground with the child helps to establish a safe and healthy learning environment.

TIPS ON HOW TO SHAPE EMPOWERMENT WITHIN CHILDREN...

- Teach children to love who they are. This includes self-identity;
- Allow children to share their opinions. Give them a voice;
- Allow children to share their talents with others who share similar interests;
- Allow children to share what they know with their parents, peers and teachers;
- Allow children to reflect their thoughts and experiences;
- Allow children to share their knowledge with others in humble ways;
- Allow children to make choices within safe boundaries;
- Allow children to self-assess their short and long term goals;
- Allow children to role-model, play act and explore (*in safe environments*);
- Allow children to dream about possibilities;
- Allow children to experiment *(build and expand their ideas, thoughts and opinions)* in safe ways;
- Ask children to always respect the space, and feelings of their peers and ask in kind ways that this favor is returned to them;
- Allow children to speak up for what they believe in just as long as they are respectful in their approach;

- Praise children when they try new things even if they fail. If children fail encourage them to try again

Resource: ***Diversity Daybook Journal***

Link: https://www.amazon.com/dp/1468145916/ref=cm_sw_su_dp

I wrote this journal for the purpose of allowing children to share their unique and diverse ethnicities as they learn about the culture, customs and traditions of others.

IT'S THERMOMETER TIME AGAIN/ REFILL THE PRESCRIPTION

FOLLOW-UP: CHECKING FOR PROGRESS

What do you do when your prescription runs out? You call your clinic/ pharmacy for a refill, right? Before you do, though, it never hurts to re-assess your progress, particularly with the child that you and your team have been focusing on. In other words, it's time to take that temperature again.

Here are some helpful tips for monitoring the child's progress:

- Pop-in on the child to observe how things are going;
- Remain in-tune and aware of what's going on in the child's school/home life;
- Gain continual knowledge of the child's perspective, interests and world views;

- Intentionally place the child in non-harmful environments to test whether he/she is using these new skills in positive ways;
- Be sure to monitor the settings and events on occasion to address potential recurrence of negative and unwanted behaviors.

A FINAL NOTE...

We've come a long way together, but always remember that this is an ongoing process. You've worked hard to 'wipe out' difficult behaviors so continue to employ the skills and tools you've learned in this guide to reinforce this progress. The 'betterment' of children depends upon the effort we expend to make it so.

Good luck!

DISCLAIMER

While every effort has been made to assist parents and educators with strategies to help students with bullying behaviors, there is no guarantee these strategies will work in entirety; however, it is the earnest desire of the author to give suggestions and examples of approaches that may help with the bullying pandemic.

Examples and suggestions are those which the author has used and/or observed other professionals utilizing during her tenure in education. Guarantees of success are entirely dependent upon the persons involved and their dedication to the tools, strategies and ideas presented within the text.

Author Motto

Love is the Key to Diversity!

Made in the USA
Middletown, DE
07 May 2022